The Language of Fragments

The Language of Fragments

LYNNE GOLDSMITH

RESOURCE *Publications* · Eugene, Oregon

THE LANGUAGE OF FRAGMENTS

Resource Publications
An Imprint of Wipf and Stock Publishers
199 W. 8th Ave., Suite 3
Eugene, OR 97401

www.wipfandstock.com

PAPERBACK ISBN: 979-8-3852-2504-0
HARDCOVER ISBN: 979-8-3852-2505-7
EBOOK ISBN: 979-8-3852-2506-4

06/25/24

For John, Robert, and Thomas, my biological brothers

Much gratitude to Jasmine Sonpar for her wisdom and very generous encouragement.

CHAPTER 1

"Billy, come into the living room. We need to talk."

"Dad," I say from the doorway, "I'm gonna do better in English, I swear. It's still early in the school semester. I'll try extra hard. I won't goof off on weekends, I promise."

"That's not what your mother and I are needing to talk about. Come sit."

I enter. Put my head back on the chair to brace for the worst. "It's not about my grades?" I say.

"No."

"Maybe I should pour you a scotch, Brent?" Mom says as she stands up.

"No, Dor"—which is short for Doris—"I'm fine. We're going to that Donaldson dinner party in an hour."

Mom walks over to her sewing basket. Takes out her sewing ring with the usual Yorkshire terrier design on it. Sits back down.

"Am I in trouble?" I say.

"Billy, what your father is having a hard time telling you—"

"I'm trying—"

"I know, Brent."

"You think you can do a better job of it?" he says.

"I'm not arguing with you, Brent." Mom looks at me and says, "It's your brother."

Dad gets up and walks over to the sidebar. Starts to make himself a drink. Doesn't turn around.

"I think I'll go wash some dishes," Mom says as she rises.

"Dor, you have to be here."

"Please tell him," she says and stops.

"What's going on?" I ask.

"Oh I forgot to call Judy," Mom says. "She wants to know what dish I'm bringing to the book club."

"That's not until Wednesday," Dad says.

"I told her I'd call her."

"Have a seat," Dad says to me.

"Dad, I'm sitting."

"Just tell him, Brent."

"You're his mother who—"

"Oh for Pete's sake," she says and rushes out. Disappears upstairs.

"It's your brother," Dad says.

"What about him?"

"He's not doing well. He got hurt—up in Oregon. He's in a coma now."

"What?"

"It was an accident. Multiple traumas. Fell while rock climbing. Has swelling of the brain. Fractures. Broken blood vessels. Close to death. His roommates tracked us down. Gave us the news."

I stare at Dad and do nothing. Then I stand, close my mouth, and leave as if nothing crazy horrible is wrong.

CHAPTER 2

MOM AND DAD KICKED my older brother out of the house when he was seventeen. They planned for him to live with Dad's brother. I was in fifth grade. They made it sound like it was some good arrangement for Paul. Something that he should like. But Paul never showed up at my uncle's doorstep. Never came back home either. And I never heard anything about him or from him as the days rolled into years. Mom and Dad said there'd be no more talk of Paul either. No more mention of his name in the house. It was like Paul fell off the face of the Earth. Morphed into some family secret that grew darker every day.

I think about my brother now as I enter Mom's sewing room. Her sewing projects scattered around. Mom in her rocking chair. Looks up at me over the top of her reading glasses. Turns off her small color TV.

"Should I come back?" I ask.

"No. Here, take a seat. You can move that over," she says of a sewing project on the couch. "I see you saw my note on your door."

"Yeah," I say. (Mom has this weird way of leaving notes instead of just saying something to my face.)

She takes off her half frames and looks at me. Smiles like it hurts. "I just wanted to review with you the talk we all had yesterday in the living room. Your father will also want to talk to you about your brother." She clears her throat. "The latest news about Paul is that there is no change in his condition, this bad state he's in."

"What does that mean? Is he going to wake up?"

"Billy, not likely. He just lies there."

"Are we gonna see him soon? Have you and Dad seen him?"

Mom shakes her head slowly.

I stand up. Face hot. Heart pounding. "You and dad are just writing him off?"

"Billy, it's not like that. There's a lot you don't understand."

"Try me. Tell me." I go stand in the doorway.

"There's nothing more to share, Billy. Nothing I can do—nothing any of us can do."

"You're just gonna let Paul die? Is that it?"

"We're not letting him die."

"Well, why aren't you and dad doing anything? Why aren't we seeing him? You say he's not getting better."

"How come?" she says.

"Yeah, don't you care about giving him a chance? We can get in the car right now and go see him. Go see what we can do for him."

"Billy, you don't understand. Your brother cut us off a long time ago."

"Uh, no . . . you and Dad did that to him. You cut him off."

"You're going to see it your own way, Billy. We understand that. And we see it our way, your father and I."

"Even if Paul made you mad and disappointed in him, you're just gonna let him drift away? Not give him any hope? Not try to help? Who's even there with him? Where is he?"

"I couldn't help but overhear," Dad says from the doorway. "I was just on my way to the mailbox."

"Help me explain, Brent."

"Billy, we're going to keep this simple. Paul provided no advance directive."

"What does that mean?"

"That means he didn't give any written directions about how doctors should handle something like the coma he's in now. He can't make decisions about his health in his current condition."

"Let's just go wherever he is to make some of these decisions for him then. Let's bring him home. He can stay with me in my room. I'll throw out my bean bag and dinosaur set to make room. I can donate those. They're old."

Mom looks up at the ceiling. Rubs her hands together.

"We haven't seen or been in contact with Paul for three years now," Dad says.

"That's not my fault," I say. "I never wanted him to go."

"We're not getting into that," Dad says.

"We're not going to be blamed either," Mom says.

"Yeah? Well, you should have thought about what you did to him. He's your own kid. You're his parents."

"Billy, watch your mouth," Mom says.

"It's your fault he's gone. It's your fault he's in trouble. He was your son. You should have loved him even if he made you mad. You should have cared!" I suddenly yell.

Dad motions for Mom to get up and leave. Just like that. They walk out. As if the conversation never took place. As if my brother Paul never even existed.

CHAPTER 3

I'M JUST A FRAGMENT. It's like the word was engraved on my forehead in big red letters or something. I'm only half there. Spaced out or something. Some part of me is missing. My eighth grade English/Language Arts teacher, Miss Snarp, constantly reminds me of this:

> "Billy, when are you going to learn? Sentences have to have verbs and subjects. Everyone else in the class has mastered this grammar rule except for you . . . "

Maybe cuz I'm a fragment I only half understand what she is trying to drill into my partial brain. To me, if there's no subject or verb hanging around, that's okay. It doesn't bother me if the subject or verb went on the lam, went running from the grammar cops. In life sometimes there is no subject, no meaning. And sometimes no verb to stir up action. Like maybe words aren't supposed to have structure all the time like Miss Snarp talks about. Where sentences get balanced or not. Maybe sentences are just supposed to ponder, wait. Maybe just hold on for life.

I look down at the two latest essays that Miss Snarp puts face down on my desk where I sit in the back corner of her classroom. (That's my assigned spot because my last name begins with the letter Y. Tail end of the alphabet.) Anyways, in one of these essays we were to describe what an apple is. Talk about stupid and boring. And then in another essay we were to write why English class is so important. It's actually not important to me. Except for this girl in

English class. She's important. Her name is Jenna. Not that I could write about that topic to Miss Snarp though.

But I flip over my essays: two grades of C. "Fragments again," Miss Snarp's comment shows in big red letters in the margin.

If you ask me, I think Miss Snarp is a fragment too. Take her classroom for example. It's one of these rooms with no windows. Nothing to stare outside at when you're bored or just want to look away. No trees or birds to watch or hear. No sky to watch the change in color, clouds, or weather. There are only weird things on the walls. Like peacock feathers, pressed and dried flowers, Japanese fans, and pictures of famous author faces. Fake potted plants here and there too on the teacher's desk and in the corners of the room. Classroom decorations plucked from somewhere else. Then forced together into this dingy room to have the remaining life sucked out of them.

Oh yeah, which reminds me: Miss Snarp says I use the "me" and "I" words wrong when I speak or write. I just figure these words are the same thing. But she's real particular. Maybe what's worse is when she goes into her parsing mode at the front of the classroom. That's when things get gnarly. That's when she breaks every word down with lines going vertical, diagonal, and horizontal. She talks crazy and fast then. Uses her pointing stick at the erase board to keep us paying attention. Says words like substantive complement, participle, adverbial clause. I have no idea what she's talking about.

But oh yeah, I haven't told you much about Jenna. The best thing in this classroom is her. She sits one row in front of me. No one else seems to notice her but me. She's quiet. Has messed-up brown hair down to her shoulders. Green eyes. Darker skin than mine. She's not tall, not thin. Almost always wears a colored tee shirt with faded blue jeans and high-top sneakers. No makeup, no jewelry. Just her.

And she pretty much keeps to herself. Lost in her own world like me, I guess. But I see her as going somewhere. Like she's got her life all together even though she didn't make the cuts for the town's middle school soccer league. At least she tried out for the team. Not something I would ever do. I've never been a jock or anything special. Just like I was too shy to say anything to Jenna at first other than a dorky comment about the school's crispier French fries one day right as she was heading into the girls' school bathroom. That's when she turned around and told me she really had to "go."

CHAPTER 4

I'M STILL WAY MAD at Mom and Dad all day at school. For them telling me once again to forget about Paul. I keep quietly drifting off into "Loser Land." I got my imaginary grammatical fragment friends there with me. All of them losers too for how they don't connect right to what's around them. Like they're denied meaning. Frag. Ment. Error of incompleteness that leaves people hanging and guessing and being rubbed the wrong way. But then I think again that sometimes things don't make sense. And that's the way life is. Like you just have to learn to live with the parts of things that you got. Like I just got a part of my brother.

"Jenna?" I say after school. I catch up to her outside on the grass.

She stops and turns around. It's my big moment to finally say something with meaning. Something super mind-blowing. But all I come up with is: "Did you do your English class assignment?"

"'You mean the importance of public speaking?'"

"Yeah, that one."

"No, I haven't started. I'm still working on the take-home quiz."

"Me neither. I haven't started. Can you believe we have to write about these dumb topics—like what's an apple? Why can't Miss Snarp just give us choices. Better yet, why can't she let us pick our own topics?"

"Why, what would you write about?"

"Me, I would write . . . I would write about how I don't care about all of Miss Snarp's grammar rules. I still have no idea what a nominative or object complement are or all the subordinating conjunctions. I just have to tune out in her foreign land of Grammar Rule World that she throws our heads into. Some of that stuff should just be used on the older kids. Like she shouldn't even mention those rules. I mean do you know what she is talking about?"

Jenna laughs. "I just memorize for the tests is all with the help of those sample quizzes."

"Wish I could say the same. Summer school is probably happening in my future. My brother was held back a year in school. It will probably happen to me too. He was no good at reading. But Miss Snarp, the grammar cop, just hates my fragments. She reminds me of my grammar crimes all the time and of how I'll never become a good writer. Who even said I wanted to be a writer?"

"And now Miss Snarp is going to randomly call on somebody in class to read their essay aloud," Jenna says.

"What?! I didn't hear that part of the assignment. When did she say that?"

"Yep. Someone will be sacrificed."

"Don't put it like that, Jenna. No. Maybe I won't show up to class all week then. Seriously, I mean I really might take off."

"And go where?"

"To see my brother."

"Where is he?"

"Up in Oregon."

"Oh."

"Yeah."

"When will you go?"

"I don't know. Should be sooner than later."

"You two are close?"

"Yeah, we were. He was—is—my only big brother. He took me places and stuff. And then he disappeared."

Jenna goes silent and then I go silent. We keep walking.

"Are you following me home?" she asks.

"Is it okay I tag along? My brother never minded me tagging along with him."

"It's half a mile to my house," Jenna says.

"Sounds good to me," I say.

10

CHAPTER 5

DAD WATCHES A SUNDAY football game. Scotch whiskey in hand. New wide-screen TV in his den. Mom bakes buttermilk biscuits in the oven as she sits in the kitchen alcove reading her *Under the Wide and Starry Sky* novel. Some thick historical romance.

"How long till the biscuits are done?" I ask.

"They'll be ready when they're ready, Billy. You must have homework to finish or start."

I go back upstairs to my bedroom and shut the door. Return to my online people search. No luck in finding my brother so far. Only one unrelated person called me back.

"Billy?" I hear Dad say.

"Yeah?"

"I want to talk. Open the door."

"I'm on the computer."

"Doing homework, I hope."

I put my computer screen on sleep mode. Get up to open the door. "Halftime, Dad?"

"Yep. The Broncos are taking out the Cowboys. Good game. You sure you don't want to watch?"

"I'm sure."

"So where'd you go last night?"

"I was with Rick. What, I can't go to a friend's house now? He has tons of video games to play. His parents are doctors. You and Mom love that."

"You got home late."

"Ten o'clock? It was Saturday."

"You know we like you home by nine. That's the rule. Also, I know we had a difficult conversation Friday—you, me, your mother."

"Yeah."

"Well, there's a lot you don't know, Billy."

"About Paul? You've said that."

"I just want you to know your brother wasn't on the best path for himself."

"You're his dad and you write him off like that?"

"Hey, show respect. Your mother and I are under a lot of stress. Give us a break."

"A break? A break from what? You're the ones going off to social parties, weekend trips. Having lots of fun."

"You think you're so smart, Billy."

"Did I say that?"

"Think you're some big shot now that you've got money in your pocket from summer jobs."

"Did I say that?"

"Well, get your own mower, get your own equipment, that snow blower you want. You have no clue about responsibility."

"Responsibility? Uh, you kicked your own kid out of the house to fend for himself and now die for all we know."

"Billy, your brother chose not to live with his uncle. You know that. Paul never showed up. That door had been open. And then he would have turned eighteen. Nothing your mother or I could have done at that point when he's of legal age, especially with us not knowing where he was."

"You didn't help him, Dad. You turned him away."

"He turned away from us, Billy."

"Not true. That's not true!"

"Fine, Billy. Take your brother's side. But Paul can take care of himself now. He made that choice. Just remember that. Hey, I got the game to get back to."

Dad heads back downstairs.

That's when I cry. I really cry hard.

CHAPTER 6

"Can I sit at your table?" I ask Jenna. She looks up from the paperback she's reading. She's sitting at one of the tables that gets rolled out in the school gym for eighth-grade lunchtime.

"I don't have to talk," I add. "I'll be quiet."

She puts a bookmark in her book and sets it down. I hand her a macramé bracelet that I made for her not long ago. Watched a YouTube video on how to do it. I give it to her like a peace offering to have her accept me. She quickly puts the bracelet on her wrist. No questions asked, no answers given.

"You going to the haunted house show?" I ask after I sit down across from her. Nervously take a bite out of my sandwich.

"Which one?"

"That scary house by Peller Hill."

"I don't know. Are you going?"

"It's open for two weeks. Closes up after Halloween. Maybe you and me could go sometime. Just wondering . . . "

"Maybe," she says slowly.

"Or maybe you like to do other things. Go to other places."

"Maybe," she says.

"Maybe," I repeat. I nervously take another bite. My fingers shaking.

Great, I think. It's only our second real conversation and Jenna already hates me.

Jenna opens up a Tupperware container. Starts eating what looks like zucchini strings. "You know a lot of people have teased me," she says.

"Teased you?"

"Yeah."

"For being bi-racial, telling me I should go back to the foreign island I came from and that I'm ugly and stupid."

"Well, that's just dumb," I say. "Neither statement about you is true. Kids are just jerks sometimes. That's the way it is."

Jenna keeps munching on her veggie strings.

"So what do you want to do?" Jenna asks as she looks around the gym at the other kids talking and eating their lunches too.

"Uh, now? You mean as far as finishing my sandwich?"

"No, I mean do you have dreams of being anything?"

"Of being somebody? Um, no. No one has ever really asked me that before."

"You've never been asked about your future?"

"Well, I must have. I just don't remember or don't think about it much. It's not that my parents are pushing me to be anything special."

"People want you—us—to figure out things, to figure out our direction in life by the time we're in high school. I hear that a lot."

"But that's four years way," I say. "I got plenty of time to figure it out by then."

"My mom wants me to succeed. She's a single mom. Tells me there are circumstances in this world that are not in my favor but then tells me to keep striving in spite of that. She believes in me."

"Cool. Yeah, I relate. I want to track down my own brother in spite of what's ahead for me. That's my goal—my goal of how I can be somebody."

CHAPTER 7

"You're leaving soon to see your brother?" Jenna says. It's our next official school lunch together. The only time we can really meet during the school day outside of English class. Jenna lets me sit across from her again. Lucky me!

"I'd skip school tomorrow but should play it safe," I tell her. "I don't want my parents to know I'm ditching. My plan is to go this weekend or the weekend after. Thanksgiving break is too far off."

"You're going alone? How can you do that? People are going to notice you're underage—just a kid. You need permission from a parent to go. Otherwise someone somewhere will report you."

"Yeah, I'm not sure yet how to do this. But my brother is hurt bad. My parents said he was in an accident. He needs my help."

"Why don't you all go together? Like as a family. By plane or by car."

"They kicked my brother out of the house three years ago. They don't exactly want to see him. They don't tell me much. Just that he's in a coma now."

"Oh. Sorry. That's way bad."

"But I have his address now and the address of an old friend of his who lives up there too. I used my parents' credit card number to get a free 7-day trial to do a people search. I checked the white pages online. Paul—my brother—that's his name—he's probably in the hospital up there. But his phone number has been disconnected and I haven't gotten a hold of his friend yet."

"Hospitals won't give out any private patient information," Jenna says. "You know that, right?"

"Well, I just want to get there. Get to the right area. His town. Know what I mean? It's only a few hundred miles away."

"I know what you mean," Jenna says. "Your big brother, you love him."

"Exactly."

CHAPTER 8

"WHAT ARE YOU DOING up there in your room all the time now? Your door closed. Billy, I want to know."

"Dad, it's my room. I sleep there."

"Don't be fresh," Mom scolds as she passes Dad the bowl of corn at the dinner table where we all sit.

"And don't talk with your mouth full," Dad says.

"But you asked me a question."

"Here, Billy, take some more pot roast," Mom says.

"No, I'm good."

"It's 'no thank you.' Your mother spends a lot of time cooking for you."

"She cooks for you too," I say.

"Billy, I said don't be fresh. That's enough."

"What do you think is going to happen if you come home with F's on your report card?" Dad says.

"Dad?"

"Answer your father."

"I don't know. I don't know what he wants me to say."

"Answer the question," Dad says.

"I'm confused," I say.

"You think everything should just be given to you, Billy? That life is just as easy and simple as you imagine it to be?"

"I never said that."

"That you can take or drop whatever you want with no bad consequence?"

"Dad?"

"Your father and I realize you don't understand a lot since you're young."

"You may think you have all the answers, Billy, but you don't," Dad says.

"So you went from wondering what I was doing in my room to now calling me a stupid jerk?"

"Your father's tired. He's had a long tough day. Best if you're respectful, Billy. Here. Anyone want more beef or corn? Fruit salad? There's more in the kitchen. We'll have leftovers for sure."

Dad puts up his hand to say no. His mouth full.

"No thank you," I say as I look down at my plate.

"You know, you better not turn out like your brother did," Dad says.

"What's that supposed to mean?" I say.

Mom gets up. Carries dishes back to the kitchen.

"Was Paul ever good by your standards?" I ask. "Because I don't remember you talking good about him."

"Be nice, both of you!" Mom calls out.

"Don't you go telling me how to run things around here. You hear me?"

"Dad, it's your fault Paul's in trouble now. It's your fault he's dying."

Dad grabs me by the collar and puts his face up to mine. "Don't you ever talk to me like that again. Do you understand?"

"Brent. Please, Brent."

Dad looks at me. Disgusted. "You didn't know anything about Paul and what he did to his life, to his future, or to us."

"Dad, you didn't know Paul either."

CHAPTER 9

"Any news about your brother?" Jenna asks on another one of our walks to her house after school. She said I could tag along again.

"Nope," I say. "This means my brother needs me asap wherever he is."

"How come your parents won't go see him?"

"They say Paul wouldn't be able to talk to them because of the coma he's in. That there's no point in going up there."

"Why don't they just get you up there then? Like give you permission and a plane ticket? Is it the cost? The time away from homework? What about a family Zoom call with someone watching over Paul? I mean I don't get it. Are your parents still mad at him that much? I know if I got in some accident—no matter where—my mom would be at the scene asap. She'd drop all her jobs. And she's a busy person."

"I know. It's messed up. My parents have nothing more to say about it. Plus, I noticed this morning that they blocked me from the Internet."

"No way!"

"Fraid so."

"Wow."

"Yeah, well, my dad thinks I'm up to no good. He treated my brother like that too. It's like he made bad things happen to my brother and then blamed him for it. Now he's cracking down on me."

Jenna stops and just stares at me blankly. I shrug before we walk on in silence.

CHAPTER 10

"Hey, I got a question," I say at the dinner table. Trying not to look scared. "Mom, Dad . . . where is Paul?"

Dad puts down his fork. Mom leans forward to pick up the bowl of carrots to pass to Dad.

"What did you just say, Billy?" Dad says.

"I just want to know where Paul is. You said he's in a coma."

"We're not going to talk about Paul," Dad says.

"Not at the table," Mom says.

"Well then, when are we going to talk about him? Is there ever a good time? Ever a good place? Do I have to be eighteen to be told anything?"

"That's enough out of you," Dad says.

"Don't start up, Billy," Mom says.

"Why, because I might end up like Paul did—kicked out?"

"You keep talking like that and there will be a consequence, Billy. Do I make myself clear?" Dad says.

"I'm just asking a simple question, Dad. I can't even ask?"

"No, Billy, it's not a simple question," Mom says as she chews her chicken fried steak fast.

"I don't get to know where my own dying brother is?"

"Maybe you should first focus on what he did," Dad says.

"What's that supposed to mean?"

I look over at Mom. Like maybe she'd help. Fat chance.

"Your brother made decisions. He chose his way of life. Your mother and I don't have to tolerate those behaviors under our roof. We make the rules here."

"What, the smoking and drinking you caught him doing? Dad, he was experimenting."

Mom shushes me.

"That's no experiment," Dad says. He knew exactly what he was doing. And you are walking a fine line here, Billy."

"Does that just mean you stop loving your son? All because he's not perfect?"

"You don't understand about love and honor and decency, Billy," Mom says.

"What do I understand then since I'm so young and supposedly stupid?" I stand up. "Paul's my brother. Please, please for once and for all just tell me where he is and what is going on."

"Sit down," Mom says.

"It's a question, Mom."

"Why do you need to know?" Dad asks.

I pick up my plate and head for the kitchen.

"Where do you think you're going?" Dad says.

"You didn't ask to be excused and you didn't finish your dinner," Mom says.

"I am finished."

"Billy," Mom says, "you only picked at your food."

"I'm not hungry."

"Good thing I got rid of your computer," Dad hollers.

I rush back out from the kitchen. "What?"

"No more computer for you. It's gone."

"What are you talking about?"

"You've been spending a lot of time disappearing into cyber world," Mom says.

"But I've homework to do."

"It's not a toy for you to play with whenever you feel like it," Mom says.

"But I need to have it in my room."

"You're getting involved with who knows what online," Dad says. "The Internet is full of terrible things. It sucks people into darkness."

"First you block me from the internet. Now you take my whole computer away? That was a hand-me-down from Rick's parents. It was mine. You know they gave it to me. And Paul, you just keep throwing him away too?"

"Fine, Billy, get your coat, yeah. Get out," Dad says. "But thank your mother for the fine meal."

I hear Mom saying something to Dad as I'm leaving. Words that I can't make out. But then I hear:

"He has no right," Dad says.

"He's only thirteen," Mom says.

"Thanks for reminding me!" I yell back to them before charging out the front door and slamming it hard.

CHAPTER 11

I TEXT JENNA. No answer yet. Some shops in town remain open as I walk around. It's Sunday evening. Snowing a little with a storm forecast for later in the week. I'm trying to calm down. Super mad at my parents still. I stop at a bench by a gas fire pit. Hood over my head as I slump down. Close my eyes. My schoolwork not finished for tomorrow. Life stinks. I fall asleep and dream . . .

I'm in this field of tall dry grass. It stretches on forever to a grey horizon. I see a plume of smoke in the distance. I'm with my brother. I'm little again, maybe seven years old. He's maybe fourteen.

"Come here," he says. "Follow me."

"Where are we going?"

"I have something to show you."

He takes off his jacket and wraps it around me. Then I see this dark three-story Gothic house in front of us. It starts to lean. Suddenly some prehistoric bird flies out of it. I scream and duck to keep from getting hit by the huge flapping wings. My brother laughs.

"That wasn't even close, Billy," he says. "Stay strong. You won't get hurt." Then he pulls me by the arm over to some wide greenish river that he wants me to jump across. It's too far to the other side and I get scared. The water starts churning and gurgling. My brother pulls me down into it all of a sudden. I don't know where I am and I can't breathe in the frigid cold. Paul laughs. I wake up all scared. Crazy dream.

CHAPTER 12

"OH," JENNA SAYS ALL surprised when she opens the front door of her house. "What are you doing here? You look beat."

"Come to see you," I say.

Jenna lets me in. First time. I see a kitchen and bedroom off to the side. Framed wall-art prints of beach scenes. Horse drawings on a round table with some charcoal stick next to the big pieces of paper. A stack of unopened mail. Take-out food containers on a counter. Empty aquarium. A CD player with stacks of CDs. A shelf of science fiction paperbacks. More shelves of different stuff.

"My mom's out working," Jenna says.

"Where at?"

"She's a plumber."

"For real?"

"Yeah, I know, people think it's weird. Like females aren't supposed to be plumbers or something—or can't be plumbers."

"No, that's cool. I know women can be whatever they want to be."

"My mom has always tinkered with things—loves taking things apart and putting them back together again. But—wait, why are you here? News of your brother?"

A white fluffy cat enters. Jumps up on a couch.

"Here, Snowflake," Jenna says. But the cat freaks as soon as it sees me. It tears on out.

"We have another cat, too," Jenna says. "Alexandra is her name. She likes to boss Snowflake around."

"My family never had any cats," I say.

"I love my Alexandra and Snowflake."

"Yeah, animals are the best to be around. We had dogs before my parents would find excuses to get rid of them. Wish I could boss my parents around. Tell them what to do and where to go."

"That's funny," Jenna says as she laughs.

"Do you think we have a chance, Jenna?"

"What?"

"I mean like for staying friends. We're getting to know each other better."

"I like that we hang out at lunch," Jenna says. "I used to sit and read by myself. Now I got you to talk with at the table."

"Yeah, I like that I got you to talk to also."

"What about your brother?"

"No news. Oh, cool you got board games. Can we play one?"

"Sure. You care which one?"

I shake my head.

She pulls out a box from a shelf and moves the drawings over on the round table. Sets the box down. Starts taking out pieces. A game I've never seen before.

"Paul, my big brother . . . he is the best," I say. "I got super lucky. I mean one time he saw some kids trying to gang up on me at a town fair. He came over and just started talking to them real nice. I don't know what he said to them exactly. But they begged him for forgiveness and left me alone.

"Another time me and him had a real bad thing happen down at this river we used to go to. The Eagle River it's called. You probably know of it."

"I've heard of it. Never seen it though."

"We found a swimming hole there. Went for a few summers. It was our secret getaway that we never told anybody about. My brother would pack the lunches. We'd hitch a car ride or two. Then he'd walk me through National Forestland. He had the place memorized in his head and the landmarks that we had to pass. Had me listen to the sounds of the river once we got there. Had me do it from different spots and in a deep pool with a waterfall. We'd put our heads in at the same time. He showed me animal tracks too and special rocks and how to make a fire to keep warm if I had to. Said he paid attention to birds because they had messages. Then he'd doze off against some big 'ol tree. Wake up and start telling me about girls and what they liked and what they wanted from guys. How to respect them."

"He knew?"

"He claimed to know. That's all that mattered to me. I mean he knew more than I did since he was my big brother—seven years older than me."

"What did he say girls wanted?"

"He said girls were looking for a guy who would treat them right. A guy who didn't think twice about being there for them, being their best friend. A guy who knew how to kiss right too. Is that what you want from a guy? Jenna, what do you want?"

Jenna smiles. "I want someone nice. Someone who tells the truth."

"That's it? A nice, honest guy?"

"Yeah. So what was the bad thing that happened to you and your brother?"

"I almost drowned. I fell in. Hit my head on a boulder and went under. Got caught in the rapids. My brother jumped in after me. Pulled me out. Saved me. Almost drowned himself trying to drag me to the shore. We never told anybody. We kept it our secret just like our river spot, a special place. Far away from everybody.

CHAPTER 13

"COMAS ARE PROLONGED STATES of unconsciousness when a person appears to be sleeping but doesn't respond to anything else going on around him." This was a sentence I wrote in some assignment for Miss Snarp. I checked to make sure that it wasn't a grammatical fragment. The essay topic was for students to write on why people should have good manners. I see lots of red marks in the margins as Miss Snarp hands back my paper during class:

> Billy, what is your thesis statement? The body of your essay shows no logical order or recognizable topic sentence. In addition, you did not address the assigned topic. I'm not even sure why you're writing about something as strange as comas or what relevance that has for anything. Is this a joke? An inappropriate joke? I don't find the humor in it. Sometimes I have no idea where you drift off to in class. Your poor attention has consequences. In addition, you have not turned in some assignments. You do, however, have time to turn things around before I determine the final grades. You can do it, Billy.
> Ms. Snarp

CHAPTER 14

THAT EVENING MY PARENTS call me into the living room again—the official Interrogation Room. I enter with dread. They sit close together on the couch—Mom upright, Dad with arms crossed. He points me to a chair as if I didn't know the drill.

"We want to talk to you."

"I figured."

"About what's going on with you at school."

"What'd I do now?"

"We got a call—"

"I swear I'll do better in English. I'll pull up my grade. Math, social studies, science class—they're all fine. I'm getting by, really."

"Billy—" Mom says.

"That's not what we called you here for," Dad says. "That's not what this is about."

"Then what is it?"

"A couple parents have come forward and informed us—opened our eyes to the grim reality that you're selling and using street drugs."

"What??! What are you talking about?"

"You heard your mother."

"Wait. Whose parents? What parents told you this? What are they talking about?"

"That's exactly what drugs do to you," Dad says. "Mess with your mind. Make you forget things, make you go crazy. A person spirals out of control under the influence of these rotten substances. I know this from my own family experience."

"Dad?"

"You're all about deceiving," Dad continues.

"What?" I lean forward in my chair ready to bolt for Jenna's place.

"We've seen the changes in you ourselves," Mom says all agitated. "Now we know."

"What??"

"You can't fool us," Dad says. "We went through this with your brother also. This is why we will be sending you to a boarding school after this semester."

I jump up out of my chair. "What?!! How can you do this? Ship me off. You have no proof of drugs."

"Parents' words are evidence enough," Dad says.

"Their words mean more than mine?"

My parents nod.

"And what's this school you're talking about?"

"It's a highly recommended institution back east," Mom says.

"East? Like the next town over? How far away are you talking?"

"Vermont," Dad says. "Three thousand miles away. It's a military academy for boys, for kids like you going down the wrong path in life."

"Wrong path? Yeah, you sure wouldn't want to keep me around here then, would you. Might as well send me all the way across the country. Get me as far away as possible. Yeah, kick me out like you did Paul. Spend money on your weekend getaways instead."

"I'm going to ignore that comment, Billy. We hardly do overnights. And your father and I will be missing you very much. Please understand that."

I laugh like this is the funniest thing I've heard since my brother squawked around in a goofy dinosaur costume. "Kinda like how you and Dad miss Paul big time?" I say. "Miss him so much now that he's wasting away somewhere and could be dead for all we know."

"Don't talk like that," Mom says.

"Show some respect for your mother."

"Did you ever think that maybe you both are 'off'? That it's not me out of whack? I'm just saying."

"If a person sinks low in life," Dad says, "he must do everything in his power to get himself back up."

"Fine. You know what? I'll be glad to go away next semester. Super glad. Far, far away from here. Far away forever. Fine by me. It's way unfair around here how I get treated, how Paul got treated."

"If that's what you think is going on around here, Billy," Dad says, "then time for you to get out in the real world and see how things really work. Time for you to grow up and be a man."

CHAPTER 15

JENNA MAKES ME FEEL better. We crack up on her bathroom floor the next night. Color each other's toenails with her mom's bright orange Halloween nail polish. Play with her two cats and their toys. Listen to one of her mom's CDs. Some New Wave band. We sip fresh lemonade that we made in the kitchen. First time I ever did that. It tastes super good.

"This is the funnest Saturday ever," I say.

Jenna laughs.

"That's funny," she says. "Wait. You hear that?"

"What?"

"Shh. The front door. Just now." Jenna turns off the music.

"No, I didn't hear anything," I whisper back.

"My mom. She's home. Hurry, put on your socks and shoes." Jenna closes and locks the bathroom door. Only one little window in here. Too small for us to escape through.

"You've told your mom about me, right?"

"Not exactly."

"Oh great. She hasn't seen me through the front windows or anything when I've walked you home after school?"

"No, not that she's mentioned. She's not always here, remember?"

"Jenna?" her mom calls out from the other side of the bathroom door.

"Oh. Hi Mom."

"You coming out soon?"

"I'm doing a facial."

"Since when?"

"Since now. I'm using your scrub." Jenna quickly opens a plastic green bottle and squeezes out goop that she slabs on her face.

"I have to pee," her mother says.

"Mom, I'm having a private moment."

Luckily me and Jenna hear nothing after that. We keep the music off. Then it's just the sound of the front door closing.

"Jenna?"

"Yeah?"

"Do I have any chance in the world of ever being your boyfriend someday? Just asking."

Jenna rolls her eyes. Then she smiles.

CHAPTER 16

I FINALLY GET A phone message about Paul! It's from my brother's best childhood friend Doug! The guy who moved from our Northern California town to Oregon in the ninth grade. Tells me he has no idea where Paul is. That he's real sorry he can't help. Says he did let Paul stay with him for six months a couple years back but that they went their separate ways. Said Paul started messing too much with drugs. Doug now lives with a girlfriend and watches out for her four little kids.

I phone Doug right back. I actually have to try his number four times before he finally picks up.

"Hey, man, what's up?" he says. "Sorry you can't find your brother."

"Me too."

"Wish I could help ya."

"You could help."

"What's that?"

"Could you just . . . tell me a good story about him?"

"Uh, sure, man . . . Let me think for a sec . . . a good story . . . Well, he could be a real decent human being, your brother."

"I know," I say.

"It's been a little while . . . Okay . . . I remember I got him to go on a hunting trip with me. Got all the gear, accessories, camo, everything. The guns loaded. We set up camp for a whole week. Rugged wilderness area. Big snow-covered peaks, forests everywhere

34

we looked. No one around for miles and miles. And then on our third morning there me and him seen these bears. Like, big bears just minding their own business. Five of them out in the meadow grazing fifty yards away. We had the perfect shot. Rifle telescopes, plenty of time to size them up, aim, shoot. We had it all. Everything. Those bears could have been ours, putty in our hands. But then bam! Your brother pulls the plug on the whole shebang."

"What do you mean?"

"Paul tells me not to shoot. Grabs me by the arm. Practically rips my sleeve off. Says it wouldn't be cool to kill these bears, that they had every right to live as much we did. Said if we killed them, we'd be affecting a whole family of bears—who knows how many— and that it'd be super cruel and senseless on our part to shoot em up. Said we shouldn't inflict pain on them like that. Said there's no sport in that. That we ought to be ashamed. Your brother never hunted one thing after that. Never even killed a fly. He made that vow."

"Dang."

"I know, wow, right? Your brother could sure surprise me sometimes."

"What else?"

"What do you mean?"

"Like anything else you can tell me?"

"Well, like I said, your brother was alright . . . I remember . . . me and him had finished the eighth grade . . . Your dad was real tough on him. Paul didn't talk much about it, what exactly went down between him and your dad. But then me and my family moved that summer. Came up here to Oregon as you know. That was going into my freshman year of high school. I didn't get to see your brother anymore. At least not for some years. But there's one thing your brother said to me I'll never forget."

"What's that?"

"He said that no matter how much your dad didn't approve of him, Paul always forgave him in the end. It was like Paul was protecting the man who crushed him, who banged up his spirit real bad. I never understood that for the life of me, Paul's turning the other cheek. Anyways, tell me what's going on with you, Billy."

"Me? Nothing. Nothing really."

"How's school?"

"It's school."

"I hear ya, man. Yeah, I never did make it to college myself. Wasn't college material. Never was. Hey, you got a girlfriend now?"

"Yeah."

"You old enough?"

"Yeah," I laugh.

"Cool, man. Things goin good with her?"

"Yeah. It's just not real official yet."

"Well, good luck with that."

"Thanks."

"Yeah, I had me some girlfriends back in the day. Oh those were the good 'ol days. Man, I'd love to go down that Memory Lane if I could. Oh hey, gotta go. But Paul's lucky to have a brother like you, Billy—someone watching out for him. You and him are one of a kind."

CHAPTER 17

I CALL DOUG BACK again that same night.

"Hey, can you tell me some more about Paul?"

"More?" his voice all groggy.

"Yeah. Like any more good stories about him. His phone got disconnected."

"Okay, sure . . . let me think . . . Uh, once me and Paul were in some Walmart. We seen this scruffy man and woman carting around a scrawny uncombed kid. Like they all hadn't changed clothes in a long time. What does Paul go and do but hurry in and buy stuff like sweaters, flip-flops, socks, a bunch of Spaghettio cans and bakery muffins. Then he waits out front of the store hoping they haven't left yet or gone out the other store entrance. He soon spots them. They're coming out with a couple half-full plastic bags in their cart with the kid in tow. Paul hands off the goods, the stuff he bought for them. They say something in another language and try to give the gifts back. But Paul won't have it. 'Take it,' he tells them. 'These are yours.' The guy nods a bunch. Then both adults start bawling. Then the kid starts crying. Then they do this bowing thing over and over at your brother like he's some king or something."

"That's my brother," I say. "I needed to hear that story."

"Hey, no problem, man."

"Have a good night."

"Sure thing. Bye, Billy."

CHAPTER 18

SNOWSTORM TO STRIKE SOON. That's what local forecasters predict anyways. That could mean fast cash for me from shoveling snow for neighbors. I could use the money. I have about $500 saved from my summer yard work jobs that I did with a neighborhood guy with pickup truck.

"Jenna?"

"Yeah?"

"There's something I need to say."

"What? Is your brother okay?" We're back in the school gym for lunch.

"It's my parents."

Jenna stops chewing.

"No, nothing happened with them. They're fine. My dad is actually busy. He's supposedly gone for the rest of the week. Some business conference."

"Did you get in more trouble?"

"Well, kinda. I mean my parents told me I'm going away. Far away."

"What's that mean?"

"My parents are sending me to a military school for boys. Like where you live with other guys and eat bad food and sleep on crummy mattresses with one blanket, and do tons of horrible boring homework and get forced into following crazy strict rules for days and nights on end with drill sergeants breathing down your neck."

"What? They can't do that—pull you out of school and force you to go."

"They're my parents. Why can't they do it? At the end of this semester. That's my parents' plan."

Tears roll down Jenna's face.

"Oh, I guess you like me," I say.

"Like how far away is this school?" Jenna says.

"Like East Coast. I know. I can't believe it either."

"And what about your brother?"

"What about him?"

"Time could be running out for seeing him. A lot of things could happen to him."

"Believe me, I think about this day and night. I dream about him even. Bad stuff and good. But what can I do? I keep trying with my parents. They don't tell me anything about Paul. I'm just a prisoner. They decide the punishments."

"I don't know." Jenna looks down at her lap. "Maybe you should run away."

"I will be running away. Soon. To find my brother. Remember?"

CHAPTER 19

"Mom? Dad? Any more news on Paul?" We're at the dinner table again. Dad is home early from his business trip. Like days earlier. "Hello?" I say. "Anybody out there?"

"We heard you," Mom says.

"You don't quit with this," Dad says.

"Dad, each passing day could mean more risks for Paul. I've read about comas."

"You've read about comas," Dad says. Sarcastic.

"What have you read?" Mom says.

"Well, Paul could be in different levels."

"Now you're an expert," Dad says.

"You should apply yourself like that to your homework," Mom says. "You could be getting all A's."

"Yeah, I'm trying to learn about the coma condition. There are different levels Paul can be in based on his original injury. But he may not pass through these levels."

"Really?" Dad says. "What are these levels?"

"He could get pneumonia or infections."

"You're a medical doctor now," Dad says.

"No, that's not what I'm saying. There are a couple ways they check people in comas. Like if they're talking or moving or paying attention."

"Well of course," Mom says, "doctors assess."

"Well, dad asked me."

"Billy, don't be putting your nose into other people's business," Dad says. "How many times do I have to—"

"Other people's business?"

"One, you're not an expert. Two, you should just forget about your brother."

I whip out of my chair. "Do you know how messed up all this is?!!"

"We know it's hard, Billy, but sometimes things in life are unplanned and unexpected," Mom says. "Now please sit down."

"Your brother made his choices. There's nothing further to discuss," Dad says.

"Oh so I should just forget about him and let him die? Just hate him automatically like you both do because he wasn't the perfect kid that you wanted?"

"He didn't try hard enough," Dad says more upset now.

"It's not that we didn't love him," Mom says. "Please sit down."

"Well, you sure got a funny way of showing it."

"You keep playing with fire, Billy," Mom scolds. "You're not thinking right."

"Playing with fire?"

"We know you're experimenting with drugs. You act out of it. If you ever get any girl pregnant—" Dad says.

"Oh God forbid—" Mom says as she drops her fork and puts her napkin to her mouth in horror.

"Miss Lotner tells us you're going over to a girl's house these days, some schoolmate of yours presumably," Dad says. "Sit down, Billy. Do as your mother says."

"Well, what does Miss Lotner know? My life is none of her business. Her and Mr. Lotner have nothing better to do than to create fake stories about everybody else in this town. But what, I'm not allowed now to socialize? Not allowed to have friends? Is that the next thing you're gonna take away from me?"

"Life isn't always about fun," Mom says. "And it's certainly not about getting whatever you want at thirteen years of age."

"What's it about then, Mom?—this life. Keeping secrets, being sour-faced and self-righteous for the rest of your lives like you've never done anything wrong? Is that it? You're both saints?"

"Enough, Billy!" Dad shouts. "Who do you think you are?"

"Was Paul even 'wrong'?" I say.

"Go to your room," Mom says. "Now."

"I'm Billy Young. Your son in case you haven't noticed."

CHAPTER 20

MISS SNARP HATES MY latest essay. No surprise there. The assignment was for students to write about a character's moral development in a book we're supposed to be reading. Miss Snarp calls it a coming-of-age story. I wrote about comas instead. Well, I actually didn't write it. This time I just copied it—turned in a whole paper that I printed out from a school library computer. An article called "The Prognosis of Medical Coma." It had the journal name, author, and date of publication right on it. It wasn't like I was plagiarizing or anything.

"Is this a joke?" Miss Snarp asks me after class on Monday morning.

"No, Miss Snarp."

"Then what is the meaning of this medical article and where did you obtain it?"

"Well, you let students use the Internet during class last week, remember?"

"Billy, what does that have to do with this assignment?"

"I came across the article there and found it of interest."

"Of interest? Billy, you wouldn't understand the medical terminology."

"Not exactly. But it got my attention."

"I really don't know what to do with you anymore, Billy. You're missing several assignments and your last couple mini-quizzes haven't met a passing mark."

"People can still recover from comas," I say.

"That's all well and good but how about you see our school counselor. How does that sound?"

"What for?"

"I'll walk you down there myself. Right now. You can have a good talk with Mr. Baldwin. He's a very nice man."

"Why?"

"Because I think that's the right thing to do. And he'll notify your parents of his recommendations. I want you to find success."

"It doesn't matter, Miss Snarp—you sending me to Mr. Baldwin. I'm not going to be here next semester anyways. You can ask my parents. I'm going away to another school."

CHAPTER 21

"I can't wait any longer," I say to Jenna. "The more time that pass-es with someone in a coma, the worse it is for them. Like they have less chance at living. But if my brother hears my voice, he'll wake up. It can happen you know. I've seen it on TV. He needs me, Jenna."

Me and her sit in a coffee shop booth after school. We're branching out from the gymnasium lunchroom. And share a soy blueberry shake that Jenna ordered.

"You realize that if you're gone overnight and your parents find out you're not sleeping over at Rick's house, they'll probably report you as missing. It'll mess you up in school too."

"I'm not doing great in school anyways. Especially in English class. Miss Snarp didn't like this morning what I turned in for our book quiz. It was photocopies. Photographed coma patients lying in hospital beds. She's still squawking about it to herself. I heard her myself in the hallway. How she said I needed psychological help."

"Well, did you tell her what those pictures meant to you?"

"What do you mean?"

"Well, I know why you're focused on people in comas, but she wouldn't have a clue about it."

"No, I never told her. Never mentioned either that those real patients actually woke up one day. Besides, Miss Snarp hates me."

"She doesn't hate you."

"No?"

"No, you're just another student to her is all. She's been teaching for twenty-four years. Her candle burned out a long time ago."

"I mean can you imagine teaching fragments for twenty-four years?" I say.

Jenna laughs. "That's funny. That's her job."

"It sounds boring as anything. No, I'm sure she'll be super glad when she hears I'm gone. How many less fragments she'll have to focus on then. She'll probably go out and buy herself some bull riding machine."

"Bull riding machine?"

"Yeah, can't you just see her on one?"

"No."

"Oh yeah. She probably hoots and hollers and twirls a lasso when she's up on one of those. Puts on some riding boots with spurs. The cowgirl hat. Blasts the country music and kicks out her legs as she rides that wild power beast."

Jenna accidentally spits out her shake she laughs so hard. "You are definitely different, Billy."

"But getting back to my trip," I say, "I can't wait any longer. It's already been over three weeks since my parents told me about Paul. That's way too long. And I have bad dreams about him still. I used to get them a lot after he was kicked out a few years back. Like he's calling out to me and I have to save him in the dream. And there's no one else there. Then I wake up in a sweat. I'm gonna ask him if I can go live with him wherever he plans to be. That's after he wakes up of course. Before you and me marry someday—I hope. I have it all planned out."

"Marry?"

"Since we get along and stuff."

"I'm not planning on getting married," Jenna says.

"Right. OK, scratch that thought. But I think we'll still be good friends for a long time. Like real long."

"But you'll be moving," Jenna says and suddenly bursts into tears.

"The boarding school prison? Jenna, it'll all be okay. We can text and skype. And we can visit with each other during school breaks. Like meet in a midwestern state. I'll earn more money. I

46

gave this all some thought. We're meant to stay together—as friends I mean. And hopefully I won't even have to go to some military academy, because my big brother will let me move in with him right away."

"I'll be getting cash soon too," Jenna says. "For reading and sending mail for a blind lady a couple streets over. Said she would pay me."

"You didn't tell me that. Cool. A job."

"But what if something happens to you?" Jenna says.

"What do you mean?"

"Like someone beats you up or tries to rob you or something."

"Like at boarding school?"

"No, on your trip to find your brother."

"That won't happen."

"There was just something in the local news about that kid getting shot at. A kid just minding his own business and walking along. It happens, Billy. These attacks."

"Yeah, but that was some crazy gang-related thing. They targeted the wrong person. I heard a couple teachers talking about it."

"Killings or attacks don't have to be gang related. They can just be from some random act. Someone doing something horrible and senseless to anyone."

"Jenna, I'm not gonna die if that's what you're wondering about. I'll be fine."

"How do you know? Today you're fine. But who knows about tomorrow. No one knows."

"Yeah, well, I'm not gonna stop trying to see my brother just because I might accidentally die along the way. That's just stupid."

"I may never see you again." Jenna cries harder.

I come around to her side of the table. "I may be leaving town, but we will be together. Just later on. We can make it happen, I know it. We can do it if you want it to happen too. And I don't want any other girlfriend. I want you."

"Girlfriend?"

"Oh sorry. That's right—friend."

CHAPTER 22

AND THEN MY LUCK turns around. Doug calls.

"Billy, hey."

"What's up?"

"You're not going to believe this," Doug says.

"You know where my brother is?"

"No, but one of my welding customers will be driving up the coast line. He said he'd be happy to pick you up if you can get yourself to the ocean. I told him a little bit about you."

"No way."

"Yes way, man."

"But wait. I don't want to make a trip if Paul's not even in your town for sure right now."

"Good point. Hey, let me see if I can get more info for you. I'll do what I can."

"Awesome."

"Yeah, I'm sure your brother would love to see you. He always talked about you."

"But Doug?"

"Yeah?"

"I got to do all this fast. My brother's life is on the line."

"I'll do what I can, Billy. Promise."

CHAPTER 23

THE DAY AFTER DOUG calls me I get this strange text:

"I know your brother. Come to 1734 Greene Lane, Cedar, Oregon. Come as fast as you can."

I try texting and calling back. No response. I look up Cedar on a map. It's a town about twenty miles east of my brother's last known address. I call Doug right back:

"Doug—"

"Hey, Billy. I was going to call you. That customer of mine had a change of plans. No drive up the coast. He's not going. Sorry, man. Hey, is everything all right?"

"Yeah, I got this weird text. You know anything about it?"

"A text? No, I don't know anything. It's not from me. What'd it say?"

I read Doug the text.

"What the heck?" he says.

"Yeah, what should I do?"

"I'd say go."

"Yeah."

"But be real careful. You don't know what you're walking into. Maybe they want money or something."

"Yeah," I say.

"You tried texting and calling the person back?"

"Yeah, like non-stop."

"You could call the cops or probably do a reverse name search online with the caller's phone number. Might cost something. I could do it for you."

"Yeah, if you can get a name, that would be awesome."

"Sure. Sure thing, man."

"I got an address now," I say. "Somewhere to go to at least. I won't wait any longer."

CHAPTER 24

TODAY I SLIP OUT. Close the house front door as soft as I can. Still dark outside before sunrise. The snowstorm never hit. But I got cash in my pocket. Duffle bag on my back. Flip phone and charger. A knit cap turned into face mask to keep me from being noticed. Snacks and Gatorade. Compass, pocketknife, matches, candle. Thermals, gloves, wool socks, extra jacket, and lightweight rain poncho packed just in case. I cut through neighborhoods. Cross town at a pretty good clip in my high-top sneakers. Stay on back roads till I get nearer to the highway going north. I keep parallel to it through a wide valley in the dim light. Not too close to the road. Then break time by lakeshore to text Jenna:

> Got a clue @ Paul. Sorry I didn't say bye. I'll be back.
> With my brother.
> Love from your FRIEND—Billy

I keep walking. I get closer to a railroad track. I keep thinking of my brother. How he would tell me things. Like when I had a bad dream I would go wake him up middle of the night. He'd tell me something super good. Like the legend of the fisherman who caught the biggest fish ever . . . The fish grew so gigantic and colorful in his hands that people came from all over the world to see it in the sea after the fisherman couldn't hold him anymore. The fish liked the man a lot. And the man liked the fish a lot. They became good friends and talked all day long.

But then one morning the fish had to say goodbye. The fish met another fish its same size and color. The pair wanted to move to deeper waters together. The man said to the fish that he would miss him. The fish said that he would miss the man too. And then they kissed goodbye and went their separate ways.

It wasn't until many days later that the man was sitting on the beach remembering his good times with the great fish and all the stories they told between each other when the old fish friend suddenly swam up to shore right where the man was sitting on a rock. Behind the fish swam five other fish, all large and colorful.

"This is my family," the great fish told the man.

And the man put his hands together and cried, "I am a happy man! Overjoyed to see you all—my Great Fish Family!"

As I walk along I also think about the letter I wrote. Left it on Miss Snarp's desk Friday afternoon:

> Dear Miss Snarp. I know you haven't liked me for a long time. Like how I write. I use fragment after fragment after fragment. Fragment. I know you want me to write something that is Whole. (I had to look up the spelling of that one.) Is there such a term in your grammar book as a Whole sentence? I guess I'm more like a hole with something missing in the middle. Something I can't get out of too. I know when I try to write whole sentences for you they don't happen. Maybe there's someone else out there who is like me. Someone who's just half there. Is that such a bad thing? A big deal Miss Snarp? Maybe some of us aren't supposed to be completed yet. Maybe that's just who we are. We're half done. We carry around halves. Like half a donut or half a burrito. I'm sorry I can't give you what you keep looking for. In my sentences. You say. Verbs or subjects missing. I can't tell you the whole verb or subject phrases. Or how to make those. Subjects, actions—how to make happen that must be magic. Pure beauty to you. Yet I'm a walking fragment. Not put together right. Top part off or the bottom half gone? I don't know. I'm lost without certain words. How to say. Sorry. But you won't have to bother with me anymore now that I'm leaving for another school. You can have your perfect English back. Your perfect class, your perfect students.

Miss Snarp. Goodbye. You tried. I tried. Maybe I'll meet
you in another life. Be happy in your ~~hole~~ whole. —Billy

I look at my breath in the cold air. Look up at the clear sky. Sun
is coming up. No Miss Snarp to look at now. Cars whoosh past in
the distance. I walk on through another valley. And then I hear it:
A deep whistle blow. The sound of a train from behind me. Loco-
motive headlights aglow from afar. Cross guards lowering, warning
lights flashing. The quick electric beep-beep-beeping sound of the
alarm up ahead. The train is going slow.

That's when I notice a guy. He's waving at me from inside the
train. From an open freight car. "Hey kid! Come on! Jump! I'll grab
you!"

"I can't!" I holler back as I'm running down a slope over toward the track.

"Sure you can. Boxcar's goin slow!"

"Going north?"

"Sure is! Come on! No time! Jump!"

The guy is right: I can catch the train. I grab a hold of the guy's
outstretched hand. He helps me up it all happens so fast. And then
he laughs and lies on his back. Huffs and puffs and sits up. Slides the
door closed part way. I look around. I can't believe it. I'm actually
inside a moving freight car. And with some guy I've never seen before. My heart pounds. I take the duffle off my back and set it down.

"Hey, hi, I'm Justin. Glad to meet you." He extends his hand.
We shake. He looks like he's from the North Pole. Bundled up head
to toe. And like he's had no haircut for ten years.

"Billy is my name," I say.

"Hey, Billy. Hey, I thought you weren't gonna make it there for
a second."

"Me too."

"Where you headed?"

"Cedar. Oregon."

What you after?"

"A dream."

"Hey, me too. "What's your dream?"

"To see my brother again."

"You love him. I can see it in your eyes."

"Yeah, he's my brother. He's been good to me."

"I hear ya."

"But he's sick," I say.

"Sick?"

"Yeah, from an accident. Hit his head. My parents said he's in a coma."

"Ooh that's bad."

"It is."

"You're all alone," Justin says.

"Yeah."

"Hey, me too. I prefer it that way."

"How come?"

"Guess you could say things haven't worked out right between me and people."

"Like what kinds of things?'

"Oh you name it. I got kicked out by family—"

"That happened to my brother too—" I blurt out.

"and lost a bunch of jobs," Justin says. "Got addicted to console games I played by myself. Never had a relationship for long."

"Sounds kinda rough."

"It was. Until I decided to make changes."

"What'd you do?"

"I stopped blaming people. Realized it didn't matter if they were at fault for some of what was wrong in my life. That it was time for me to change myself, change my reactions. What I mean is my family never liked me, never approved of me. They always told me and other people that I had a mental disorder. That I would never amount to much—"

"Like my brother," I blurt out again. "My parents didn't approve of him!"

"—but instead of feeling sorry for myself, I finally decided to tell myself I'm likable and that I can still be who I want to be and do the things I want to do."

"Yeah, there's always someone out there in the world who can like you, for sure. I have a friend like that now. Her name is Jenna. She likes me a lot. You have friends now?"

"Yeah, I got me some. And on top of that, I'm living the life I want."

"What kind of life?"

"I'm a bookkeeper. I handle business accounts online mostly. Taught myself and started my own business. I'm good at it."

I high five Justin.

"Yeah, I've built people's trust. They put up with my hair. If only my family could see what I've made of myself."

"You're proud."

"I am. So what got you all the way out here by yourself?"

"My parents didn't want to help me. They don't care about saving my brother. Not like I do. I haven't seen him for three years."

"That's a long time."

"Yeah, my dream is to wake him up from the coma he's in. For him to hear my voice . . . "

And then me and Justin just go quiet. We stare out at the forest we're passing through. I see a pond and geese flying overhead.

"What got you hopping a train?" I ask.

"For the sake of beauty."

"Beauty?"

"For connecting with possibilities and solitude. Nature and machinery. For taking personal risks where life and danger dance together."

"Whoa, that's deep."

"Life isn't about my job, how much money I make, or whether people accept me or not. It's not about their opinion of me or how their meanness impacts me. It's about finding beauty in the things that I don't know, have yet to explore," Justin says. "That's how I'm living my life now."

"'That sounds cool. And super scary too. I'm like you. My fear is I won't get to my brother. But the beauty would be in finding him."

"The journey of discovery based in love in spite of fear," Justin says.

Then me and him just go quiet as we look out at more of a canyon landscape that we're passing through. It's a pale morning sky streaked with wispy clouds. We hear the clickety-clack of the long train pulling its weight. We're on our way somewhere through mountains and valleys. Some place unknown. I ask him if he wants some of my Cheetos. His eyes are already closed.

CHAPTER 25

I SNACK AND DRINK and watch the changing scenery while Justin sleeps with his head on his tied sack. I cover myself with my extra jacket. The train winds along past hills and a river now. I see deer and coyote.

"Where's your home?" I ask him once his eyes are open again.

"South of here. Drapersville."

"You scared of getting stuck going too far from home? Or getting caught?"

"The chances exist."

"How will you get back home?"

"Another freight train."

"Does this train go right to Cedar? Does it stop there?"

"The beauty of not knowing," Justin says with a smile.

"Well, I think I'll look for some road signs to read if we get close enough again to a road. I have a couple online maps I brought. I'll just have to take my chances where I get off."

"That's right," Justin says with a smile again.

"Hey, I was wondering . . . You said you had a mental disorder. What does that mean exactly?"

"When I was younger, I didn't talk much. Supposedly didn't talk to anybody. 'Mentally disturbed' was the label people gave me. But I had a fascination for trains. I would get train books out at the public library. Anything I could find that had to do with trains. Kids teased me for all the nerdy facts I knew. They called me weird for wanting to learn about something they viewed as totally insignificant. Hey, I'm fascinated by trains. I don't know why. Maybe I was a train engineer in a past life. Who knows. But the sight, sound, and feel of trains fills my soul."

"Then you got your wish," I say.

"I did," he says. And smiles.

CHAPTER 26

JUSTIN STAYS ON THE boxcar. Me, though, I jump off into a pile of gravel by an auto body shop and tractor lot at the edge of some little town.

"Take care of yourself!" he calls out. "You took a chance, Billy!"

"Stay out of trouble!" I call back to him.

He waves hard and fast at me as the train pulls away out of sight. I stand and wave back with all my might too until I can't see him anymore. I feel bad he's all alone. Like my brother, I think. But then I tell myself Justin likes it that way. Just him and his trains. I quickly text Jenna: "I just rode a freight train with some guy who taught me all about life!"

"Is this Kulver?" I soon ask a nice-looking lady filling her tank at a gas pump.

"No, but I'm headed in that direction. You need a ride?"

"It would help," I say as I put a folded map back in my duffle.

I hop into her car. A silver SUV. Way clean. I ride buckled up in the passenger seat. Her son behind me. Seat facing backwards. He pipes up every now and then all excited. Repeats the words "sippy cup" or "hi mommy" or "doggie, doggie."

"What's in Kulver for you?" she asks me.

"Oh it's just some place I need to get to. You can drop me off at the high school there if that's okay. If you know where that is."

"You got friends or family there?"

"I'm headed to see family, yeah."

"I never pick up strangers in my car, but something tells me you could use a little help. What grade are you in?"

"I'm just a kid," I say since I don't want to flat out lie that I'm seventeen years old. She's a nice lady.

"Yes, I can see you're young."

I want to ask her her age too but figure that's impolite. She doesn't look over twenty-five if I had to guess.

"Oh here are some flyers if you're interested," she says.

"Flyers?"

"Announcements. Tucked right down in here. About a low-cost Thanksgiving meal at the town hall. There'll be a raffle too. People can win prizes like a handmade quilt, a free car wash, tickets to a theatre production by local high school students—all of it donated. It's a lot of fun and raises money for our homeless shelter."

"Nice," I say.

"Petey, I'm putting on your favorite music," she says as she looks back at her son. "It's a CD of lullabies. He just loves it. He'll be asleep in five minutes. Just watch. You got to learn the tricks of the trade—I mean tricks to comfort your kiddos."

But me, I'm thinking her kid is already calm. He's not bawling or screaming or lobbing his sippy cup at me or anything.

The mom looks over at me again. "I'm sure your mom had or has her techniques too?"

"Sure," I say.

"I have another one on the way—baby, that is."

"Oh?"

"Indeed, I'm four months pregnant."

It doesn't show on her, some belly bulge, but I don't say anything.

"This will be my second. I want three more. Three more babies."

"Oh," I say again, not knowing exactly what to say.

"Little Petey back there is such a nice-tempered little guy. We really lucked out. He could have been a hellion."

I don't know what hellion is, but I figure it's bad because it's got the word hell in it. I figure me and my brother Paul are hellions because my parents didn't—don't—ever want us around.

"I really want for him to have another brother," she says.

"No girl?"

"Well, I come from a family of five girls. This time around I want all boys in the picture. Besides, girls are different."

"Yeah, they sure are," I say.

The lady laughs. "What's your mom like?" she asks.

"My mom?"

"You do have one?"

"Yeah. She's a lady who, like you, has things together."

"Together . . . "

"Yeah, well, she goes to a book club and a sewing group and takes care of the house. Shops, cooks, cleans. Stuff like that."

"A house manager."

"I guess."

"Meaning an overworked, underappreciated, and unpaid caregiver," she says with a smile. "You like your mom?"

"Like her? Yeah, she's my mom."

"That doesn't mean you necessarily like her. I just hope my two babies grow up loving me. I want to give them the best in life that I can."

"You're a good mom," I tell her.

"How would you know?" She looks over at me with a smile.

"I can just tell."

"Tell my husband that. Sometimes he looks at me like I'm from another planet, like when I do my baby talk to Petey."

"Naw, that's just a perfect example of you being a good mom."

"Thank you," she says. "Thank you. You know, it's tough. Hard to always know if you're doing the right thing or not for your baby."

"What about parenting books?"

"I don't have time for extra reading. I'm still trying to figure out what to feed my family every day and night for meals. Deciding on the weekly menus, buying items, ingredients, doing prep work and breastfeeding in between taking care of my husband's mother who also lives with us in our basement—with her different dietary needs and my husband's diabetes. Have to be careful what I put on their plates."

"Sounds way hard."

"It is, but I love it. It's what I chose. What about you? What are some of your roles in your family?"

"Roles? . . . I hate being me sometimes," I finally say.

"Oh no!"

"Yeah, but right now I just want to find my brother. That will make me feel like a better person."

"You don't know where he is?""

"Not exactly."

"I sure hope you find him," she says.

I text Jenna after: "Just got a car ride from a super nice mom with her little kid in the back seat. I'm in Kulver! Check the map!—Billy"

CHAPTER 27

I'M ON FOOT AGAIN. Farms and fields all around. All I can think about are Jenna and Paul. As many good memories as I can fill my head with as I walk across a two-lane bridge . . . *like how Paul would bring home some of his baseball teammates after their little league games. They'd be all dusty, scuffed up. Mom would set out milk and snacks for them on the kitchen table. They'd laugh and tell stories. Talk about their recent game and team players or the American League. Paul had me sit with them. Like I was one of them.*

They'd all head for the tree house in the backyard once the food was gone. I was the guard who kept watch of the loft hatch while they played their card games and talked mostly about girls and sports, music, and movies. I colored in my snake and lizard coloring book. Soaked up whatever they said.

Sometimes the guys would bet candy or baseball cards during their games. The winner got to take the prize home or else leave it for betting the next time around. A couple times Paul snuck up liquor from Dad's side bar and gave me a sip too. One time an owl even came to check us out. It was our larger-than-life treehouse up in what seemed like the tallest of trees . . .

And then I think about Jenna. How I miss her. I take out my phone and dial her number.

"Any boy trying to date you yet?" I ask her.

"That's funny," she says and laughs.

"I'm serious," I say.

"Where are you? Are you okay? Any news of your brother?"

"No, but I'm a hundred and something miles away now. Getting closer."

"Any more texts from Cedar?"

"No."

"I was thinking," Jenna says, "what if that person who texted you was playing some joke on you? Like wasn't telling you some truth about Paul."

"I have to take a chance, Jenna."

"Hey, you want a horse?" some woman's voice calls out to me from across the road. She's petting the animal over by an apple tree. Fenced pasture. Bucket on the ground nearby. She's in mud waders.

I wave at the woman. "Gotta go, Jenna."

"Okay, bye. Call me later."

I cross the country road.

"I got me a couple horses I'm trying to sell. The older one's in the stable over yonder. Both mares born and bred right here. You look like a horse person."

I come up a little closer to them. Put my hands on the fence. "Nope," I say. "But what's a horse person look like?"

"You. You just look like you could speak their language."

"Nope. Never talked to one in my whole life. But my girl-friend's mom has probably talked to horses. She draws them with charcoal. I know she likes them a lot."

"That's a shame you're not familiar. Do yourself a favor and ride a horse someday. Get to know one. That's my advice. This here horse and another I have were actual therapy horses."

"Therapy?"

"You bet. Horses are attuned to people. They pick up on human energies, human emotions. They don't need any words. No conversations. They figure you out just as soon as you get in their presence. Hey, let me give you my produce business card. If I still haven't sold both horses, your family members are welcome to make an appointment to see them for yourself. Just have them drop me a line if they're wanting to come by. We can arrange something."

"Why you want to sell them?"

"These are tough times," she says.

"These horses, they must be attached to you."

"They are."

"They sound like miracle horses."

"Yes, they are. And they've liked their home here as far as I can tell. I just can't afford them anymore. Had some big vet bills last month."

And then out of the blue I ask her something that surprises even me. "Would you sell the horses if they were your brother or sister?"

"Excuse me?"

"Would they matter to you then?"

"They matter to me."

"Not enough," I say.

"You got a point there," she says.

"Animals have feelings too," I say. "They need you. They're family."

"Like I said, you got a point. I'll see if I can hang on to my babies. See what I can do. She pats the horse on the side. Come on, Ginger," she says. "Let's get you back in."

CHAPTER 28

I KEEP ON. THE scenery changes again. I'm tired. Feet sore. But have to fight it. I finally get to some historical mining town. Plop down on a wooden bench inside a remodeled one-room schoolhouse—now a bus depot. I'm the only one here. Finally warming up. I eat potato chips and Cracker Jacks and drink lemonade that I just got from the general store on Main Street. A handwritten taped note at the depot counter says the clerk will be back at 2:00 pm and then will leave at 4:00 pm. It's past 2:00 pm. I see a few bus schedules on a foldable table nearby. The next and only bus isn't arriving and leaving until one in the morning. It's a bus I need to take.

I think of fragments again. But this time I think of them in a good way. How fragments are a start of something. How they're making their way towards understanding. Too bad Miss Snarp can't make friends with the lonesome fragments hanging out all by themselves.

And that's when I see and open Jenna's text that says, "Your parents called my mom's house."

I take some deep breaths. Try to calm down. Plug my phone into a wall jack and call her.

"How'd they get your house number?" I ask.

"From talking with Miss Snarp who knows we do school lunches together. She's wanting to meet with you."

"Miss Snarp?"

"Yeah, and you must have left her a letter? Wrote of suicide?"

66

"What?! What is Snarp talking about? I left that letter in her box after school yesterday. It never said anything about suicide. She's cracked."

"All I know is that people are asking about you. You might even get in the local news if school admin told cops you're missing and supposedly suicidal."

"Great. They reported me to the cops?"

"I don't know. I just know that word is out."

"That's just great. And now my parents know your mom?— Not like my parents ever texted or called me or anything about Miss Snarp's reaction to my letter. Not that they checked on me for themselves when I could be in danger. No, they wouldn't do that— wouldn't call me. Heck no. But I didn't know this would all happen so fast. I thought I'd have a full day to get ahead of everybody and anybody."

"Yeah, cops may be looking for you right as we speak. They can probably track you by your phone, you know."

"I doubt it. There's no internet on it, no GPS. But let's get off anyway. I'll try to change my looks a little. Chop my hair. Get my winter cap back on. I'll call you back when I can."

"Okay," Jenna says, her voice scared.

CHAPTER 29

I DOZE OFF ON the depot bench. A woman's voice wakes me up:

"Oh my God, oh my God. You're just like him. My baby. My boy. Spitting image," she says. She sets down her shoulder bag and bus schedule.

"Excuse me?"

She stares down at me. My eyes half-closed. Head cap rolled up to my forehead. She's in clunky boots and woven poncho.

"I swear to God you're the reincarnation of my son."

She reaches out and touches my hoodie sleeve with her fingers all shaking. I sit up.

"I've been praying for some visitation, some kind of reminder of my son's presence. He's not coming home. I knew he'd never make it back—not back here alive anyway. Overseas . . . senseless war. I just had this feeling. Mother's intuition. It'll be another holiday without him. I'm heading to my sister's bungalow for two weeks." The woman sits down on the bench across from me. Leans forward. "How old are you?"

"Almost a high schooler." I reach for my duffle bag.

"No, no, don't go. Please. I don't mean to scare you. Just let me look at you. Can I tell you about my son? Would you let me?"

"Okay. All right."

"Thank you. That means a great deal to me. I'll begin with the day he was born . . . my baby was just the most beautiful thing I ever saw. Tiny toes, fingers. Face all puckered up. Sleeping and feeding,

68

feeding, feeding. Thought he might break in my hands. So delicate. I had no idea how I was going to take care of him after my husband ran off. He was the breadwinner. I had a whole new life ahead of me to figure out. But Ray. That was my baby's name. Like a ray of light. That boy, he put me through all kinds of emotions. Some I didn't know I had." She chuckles. "I cleaned up my act because of him. My boy made me want to live again. Made me want to sing again. I rediscovered my true calling all because of him. I sang him lullabies.

"And singing I did. Got me a job at a cocktail lounge and been singing ever since. Even came close to a recording contract some years back. Never happened though. No big loss in my life—that one. Not like the news I got of my son. A knock at my door from the United States military. How he was gone. I mean gone. That was the bomb that hit and wiped out my world."

She looks down and weeps. "I never should have started my rants, never should have had spats with my Ray. The harsh words between us. Terrible. And all for what? What purpose did it serve? And everything he went for in his life when he got older—his goals and dreams—if it meant he'd have to go far from me, then I told him he shouldn't pursue those dreams, that it wouldn't work out. I would hold him back all for the sake of me, what I wanted, how I wanted him near me . . . He hated me for that in the end. Hated the control. That still didn't stop me though. I'd put my foot down even more when he showed more signs of independence. He told me how crazy I was, how I watched his every move. I was crazy. I never realized my loneliness, insecurity, the reassurances I needed in life from those I loved . . . Never did remarry.

"I hurt my son, my not letting him go." She sobs. "I was a bad mother. Didn't want to look in the mirror and see my own fears. Believed he was all mine, that I couldn't share him with others who were getting his attention and love. He follows me, stays at my side still. Whether for comfort or punishment—or both—I don't know. But I do believe it—that he's there—here. I feel him, his presence. Sometimes I think I even hear him breathing. I reach out. But nothing. Nothing in the air to hold onto. How could I have turned him away? Made him run from me. He enlisted in the army to escape. That's what he did. To get away from me. I know that now. I drove him to his death. It was all my fault. My fault he died in some insane war."

"Maybe you just did the best you knew how," I say. "There aren't manuals out there on how to be a human."

"No, I killed him, that's what I did. No matter how much I look at it, I took his life away."

"Did he ever write you?"

"Write me?"

"Like letters when he was in the army?"

"Yes."

"Okay then. That's a sign right there that he still loved you. There's no better sign than that."

The woman cries some more.

"That shows he took time to give you his attention. He shared with you. He told you things, personal things."

"Why yes, yes, he did."

"He could have been watching Gomer Pyle reruns online, but no, he took time to talk with you. If he'd never wanted you in his life anymore, then he wouldn't have written."

"True, true. You got a point there. And the letters he wrote . . . they did tell me a lot about how he was doing—his living conditions, different village people and their cultures . . . "

"Yeah, see, he wanted you to know. He put you in his life—you were a focus for him for a reason. He chose that."

The woman keeps crying.

"Oh you're a good-hearted soul. Just like my son. He wanted to help. He wanted to protect. He wanted to serve his country. That's why he went off to fight for humanitarian reasons. It wasn't all an escape from this needy mother of his."

"I have a brother I want to help too, want to protect."

"Do you? My apologies, goodness. I've only been talking about myself. Shame on me. And I'm just some stranger to you, some lunatic mother. Tell me, do tell me about you—your life."

"Don't be sorry. I know what it's like to hurt."

And the woman looks at me all soft. "I bet you do," she says.

"I'm not exactly sure where my brother is. But I worry that he can't wake up from a sleep he's been in after having been knocked out in an accident," I say. "It's been days. His unconsciousness. He's lying down somewhere and I don't know who's there to help him."

"He's in need of critical care," the woman says.

"He is, but he's not in pain supposedly."

"That's fortunate news."

"Yeah, he just needs me in his life like when I needed him. He was always there for me. Now it's time I wake him up. Time I take him home. Wherever he tells me to go."

"Your brother loves you."

"Yeah, he does. He always did. Just like your son loved you, ma'am."

"Yes, he did in spite of all I did to him, how I crushed his soul, tried to hold him back," the woman says with her face scrunching up before crying some more. Then she looks at me. "Don't ever let him go, your brother," she says. "I mean let him go—accept him for who he is—but love your brother till the end."

"Oh I will. I do. I'm going now to tell him that—that I love him. And that he'll always be wanted. I will never walk away from him. Hey, you got an extra scarf on you by any chance?"

CHAPTER 30

I THINK OF MY family. Like when things went bad . . .

"I'm always in trouble," Paul says to Mom and Dad at the dinner table one night. "It's not fair."

"Your report card, Paul. You deserve to be grounded for that."

"Well, I scored three lacrosse goals on Monday."

"And?" Dad says.

"It's a super big deal, Dad. My team gets to go to the league playoffs now."

"Paul, a swelled head—"

"I'm good and I helped the team," Paul interrupts Dad. "Just ask any of the guys I play with who's the best player in the league and they'll all point to me."

"There's more to life than lacrosse in the sixth grade," Mom says.

"Not to me right now there isn't," Paul says.

"Don't disagree with your mother."

"I'm just saying."

"Egotism is pure vanity," Dad says.

We all pause before eating again. I don't know what Dad's words mean but I know they're not good. I try to finish my dinner fast. I kick Paul under the table, jerk my head to the side a couple times to tell him to finish up fast and get out of here, out of the room. I don't want Dad mad. But what does Paul do? Speaks up again:

"Those two neighborhood friends of yours—Mr. Winkler, Mrs. Boder. I saw them making out. Right in her parked car."

Mom sets her fork down.

"Did I just hear you right?" Dad says.

"They're married, Paul. You're mistaken. Please show some respect," Mom says with a shaky voice, eyes lowered.

"They could be criminals or celebrities for all I know. But they were sucking face."

That's when Dad grabs Paul by the shoulder. "Stop. Stop with your filth—"

"It ain't my filth!" Paul says.

"It's spreading bad rumors, Paul," Mom says.

"Not my fault those two aren't good at sneaking around. Everybody on the street has figured out what they're up to."

"Did you hear what I said?" Dad says.

"They're your friends, Dad, not mine."

Dad grabs Paul by the collar now. That's when I dive under the table. Hunker down.

"Billy, get out from under there. You're not a dog," Mom says.

But for some reason I start barking. I hear a plate break overhead. Next thing I know Dad is wrestling Paul on the floor. Paul is crying. But then Paul stops, like he gives in all of a sudden to Dad. I can't remember what all happens after that, but I bark and Mom yanks me out from my hiding place, gripping and shaking me by the upper arms to snap me out of it, but I can't stop. I cover my ears, close my eyes. Disappear and bark.

CHAPTER 31

I GET REAL LUCKY. I convince some wrinkly balding guy in overalls to help me get a bus ticket before he buys his own. Tell him my whole story about how I'm going to see my sick brother and needing to get there fast. Don't think he understands English too good, but I show him my cash. He buys me the ticket right before the clerk's closing time. I pay him back for my ticket and hand him $20 extra for his help. He likes that. We get on the bus together later like we're related.

He sits right behind me now. His overhead light off. He's got an old quiet chihuahua in a pet carrier bag on the seat next to him. Middle of the night now. My head against the window. My hood up and covering part of my face. I doze off.

"Hello," some big-cheeked roly-poly guy says to me after boarding later.

I grunt. No longer asleep.

He wears coke-bottle glasses and holds out his puffy hand for me to shake in the dim light. I give him a soft fist bump. He flicks on a little keychain light beneath his chin to flash me a grin. The light hangs from some ribbon necklace he wears with jangling plastic baubles and metal tags. He forces his piece of luggage into the overhead rack. Squeezes himself in beside me. Switches on the overhead reading light. Munches on a half-eaten Snicker's chocolate bar still in its wrapper.

"Right on time," he says all cheerful as he looks at his big wristwatch and takes in a deep breath. Pops a couple pills in his mouth

74

from a bottle he takes from a pocket. Wipes away sweat from his forehead with a handkerchief. Takes out a worn, thick paperback from his coat pocket.

"It's a regular page-turner," he says to me. "Moby-Dick. Keeps me up at night. Ever read it?"

I shake my head.

The passenger in front of us turns around and tells him to be quiet—that it's three in the morning.

"Amazing book," he says to me in more of a whisper. "This captain guy wanting revenge on a whale and the lengths he goes to kill it. As if the whale is pure evil. But it's his own plotting ways for power that do him in. I already know the ending."

"You're not an English teacher, are you?"

"No, why?"

"Oh nothing. Just wondering."

"No, I just like to read the classics when I'm not doing computer programming—i.e., correcting errors, conducting trials, storing data, investigating networks—yawn, yawn, yawn."

"You must make good money."

"I do all right. It helps that I don't have family to take care of. It's just me and my bird McPhee."

"Bird? What kind of bird?"

"She's a rainbow lory. Best little darlin. Have had twelve splendid years with her. Phenomenally acrobatic and loving. Quite the clown. Even talks to me. Asks me what I want to eat and then tells me I'm 'full of it.' Says 'Gesundheit' when I sneeze. She imitates the neighbor's cat too."

"A regular little comedian," I say.

"Yeah, she's quite the entertainer and calls out to me by name —'Benjamin, Benjamin, Benji boy.' Repeats my 'lory love' phrase that I use with her. Lory love, lory love."

This Benjamin guy finishes eating his candy bar and licking his fingers. Takes out another big chocolate bar from his shirt pocket. Rips open the wrapper and lets it drop to the floor like he did the last one. Starts chomping.

"This is my—let's see—fourth King Size Snickers bar in the last—" and then he looks at what he calls his cool G-Shock wristwatch before stating with mouth full—"forty-four minutes and twenty-one seconds. I can't get enough of these candy bars."

Should have gotten me a wristwatch and keychain light back in the old mining town when I had the chance, I think to myself, as I stare at Benjamin's wristwatch.

"You ever go wild and branch out into Milky Ways, Twix, Crispy Crunch, or Krackel?" I ask.

"Occasionally I eat the 3 Musketeers bars. You?"

"Me, anything chocolate is cool—Mounds, Almond Joy, Nestle Crunch, Reese's—whatever."

"Yours is not a discriminating palette," he says.

"Guess not. Hey, does this Moby guy lose everything on his journey?"

"Moby-Dick? He's the whale," Benjamin says. "But the captain is Ahab. Why, you gonna read it?"

"A book like that? That long? No way, Jose."

"Well, then I'll tell you about it if you're up for hearing. I've always been a night owl. Can chatter or read till the sun comes up. This here book . . . This commander guy, this character, goes maniacal. He pins his whole life on destroying this whale that robbed him of his leg. Blames the whale for his pain, plus everything else that's ever happened to anybody since the dawn of time this guy blames the whale for. I mean the guy is not your mentally stable joe. He does everything he can to avenge the whale to get payback for what he's suffered on account of the whale. The irony, the tragedy or beauty of it all, if you will, is that the behemoth, the whale, kills him in the end—takes the captain down into the depths of the ocean along with him. It takes the author about a million pages to get to that point in the story, but it happens. The whale supposedly lives."

"That sounds like reading torture to me," I say. "The author can't get you there any sooner? Can't get to his point?"

"Hey, it's Melville, come on."

"Sorry, I don't know the guy. I don't really read unless I have to."

"I hear ya. I used to be that way until one day I woke up and all I wanted to do was read read read. It didn't matter what text I put my eyes to. I just felt like I'd missed out too long on other people's stories. I had this revelation that I'd been asleep for twenty years, figuratively speaking. You ever get that way?"

"What, feel like I'm asleep? Out of it? Yeah, English class does that to me."

"Hey, it's hot in here. You hot?"

"Nope. Hey, you know anything about comas?" I say.

"Comas? No, why?"

"Aw, nothin. Just wondering."

The guy works at getting his coat off as he stands up. But then he's got nowhere to put the coat except for on his lap.

"Can I ask you a question?"

"Sure," Benjamin says. "Don't know if I can answer, but . . . "

"Why'd this captain go crazy over a gigantic animal that has a mind of its own and lives in its own watery world? I mean isn't the guy barking up the wrong tree?"

"Yeah, right? But it's like he's crazy, at least way overboard—no pun intended—in his intent on killing this one objectified thing, as if the whale's demise will free his own human life. He's just eaten up by bitterness and hatred and the drive to destroy at all costs. The irony is that these—his own emotions, his self-sabotage—are what kill him in the end."

"He's a loser in the end is what you're saying. Kinda like a fragment," I say.

"What's that?" Benjamin says.

"Oh nothing. But my brother would like the fishing part of the story, the battle to reel in a big whopper. At least before he went pro-animal. But what's the point of the tale?'"

"For me," Benjamin says, "it's all about proverbial blindness. Getting so caught up in yourself that you can't see well enough about what's going on around you. Can't see the forest for the trees."

"Then it's not about fighting for what you think is right?"

"It is that, sure. But what does this guy get in the end by trying to prove himself? What's his triumph? His redemption? Is he even justified by the mission he undertakes?"

"He sounds off his rocker," I say, "like he's got bats in his belfry big time."

77

"However you view the story," Benjamin says, "it gets you thinking, right?"

"Yeah, I guess. Though me, I'd wanna be the fish."

CHAPTER 32

I HAVE A LOT to think about on the bus ride. I doze in and out. Excited and scared. Not sure what's ahead. But I don't want to end up like Captain Ahab—full of bitterness. Makes me think of Mom and Dad. The gloom they carry around. Their grudge towards Paul rotting them out. I think of the counselor my parents dragged me to. Counselor Jim they called him. Some psychologist guy. He was also an ordained minister or priest. That's what my brother Paul told me about him when I was older anyways. I don't know why I was made to see the guy or how many times I went. But I do remember Counselor Jim had this big doghouse in his office. It had red trim on it. A doghouse I liked to crawl into. I now have this dream:

I'm in the doghouse. Barking. On my side. My back towards Counselor Jim. He sits cross-legged on the floor outside the doggie door. He's looking in at me when I turn around. I stare at him.

"May I come in?" he says. His voice all nice. He jiggles Horse puppet on his hand.

I bark at them both. That's all that comes out of my mouth.

"What's it like in there?" Horse asks me.

I bark some more and kick up one leg in the air. I'm wearing snow pants, snow coat, moon boots. Mittens with attached string through coat sleeves.

"Can I come in?" Horse asks me.

I bark back.

"I wish we could be friends," Horse says.

I look hard at Horse. I stop barking.

"I live nearby," Horse says.

"Nuh-uh," I say.

"We just haven't talked yet," Horse says.

I shake my head and wave him off.

"I'm sad," Horse says.

"Nuh-uh." I turn on my back and suck my thumb.

"Well, I'm Giraffe and want to meet you too." Counselor Jim jiggles Giraffe at me from his other hand.

"Nuh-uh," I say as I wave off Giraffe.

"I like to talk with friends," Giraffe says. "I hope we can be friends."

I grunt, scrunch up my face, stick out my tongue. Pound the floor with my boot soles. I don't stop.

"You are mad indeed," Giraffe says.

I bark but this time on all fours. I face him. This time I'm fierce.

"Yes, you're very mad," Giraffe says.

I sit back. Fling upward kicks in the air towards Giraffe.

"Sometimes when I get upset," Giraffe says, "I talk with Horse."

I shriek and stand up in my doghouse. Walk around in a tight circle. Quiet. Stiff arms down at my sides.

"I tell Horse my feelings," Giraffe says. "Horse is my friend."

I cover my ears. Put on my mittens. Cover my ears again. Walk in a tight circle. Arms stiff. Stare down at my boots. I like that they're all big and warm. Like how they'll carry me through any storm.

"I wish we could talk," Giraffe says.

I ignore him and go into a back corner. Face away from all of them.

"Maybe someday you'll let us in," one of them says.

I go to shake my head but stop. Let them figure it out.

"I think next time Doggie will show up," one of them says to me. "Doggie would love to meet you. Would that be okay?"

That's when I scrunch down into a ball. Rock slow and suck my thumb. I hide.

And then the dream fades.

CHAPTER 33

AND THEN I DREAM some more . . .

I'm with Paul. We're by some valley river I've never seen before. Mountains in the background. Water moving slow. Eagle flying overhead. My brother holds this fish that sparks and sparkles different colors when he turns it in his hands. The fish feels soft like rabbit fur when I touch it. Paul places the fish back in the river that thickens and turns the color of gold. He puts his arm around me. We walk along the gravelly riverbank. Hear part of a song he once liked. Music coming from the bristling trees. Coldplay's 'Beautiful World' song from CDs that Paul once found in the woods and played over and over. My brother turns to me. Says something like how he used to rule the world until he saw a sea of stars. That I was his sky and he wanted to be my earth, and that he didn't understand. Said it didn't turn out as he had planned. Said I won't slip out of his brotherly hand.

CHAPTER 34

I SIT UP TALL. Stare out the bus window. I down a couple bags of Cheez-Its, couple boxes of Cracker Jacks, and Benjamin's King Size Snickers bar that he gave me. Wash it all down with green Gatorade. The bus driver announces my stop at a place called Plum junction. I say goodbye to Benjamin. He slips his paperback in my duffle pocket. Insists I take it. I say okay and thank him.

Last part of my trip now! Probably around 50 degrees outside in the sprinkling rain. Grey sky. Hills in the distance on both sides of the two-lane highway with no cars in sight just yet. No houses or businesses either. Feels like I'm in the middle of nowhere again. Road sign says Cedar 23 miles ahead. I picture myself like the Moby Dick whale that Benjamin talked about. Whale who found freedom. I walk through a valley. The road curves off at the end in a grove of trees. I text Jenna how close I am now to seeing my brother. That nothing can stop me. Jenna calls me right back.

"You're sooo close," she says. "Have you tried calling or texting that Cedar number again? See if you get any response this time?"

"Yeah, good idea. I've tried a hundred times before but maybe now someone will answer. Maybe they were busy or something. You're right."

"Oh and Billy, Miss Snarp—she wants to help you pass English class."

"What? How do you know that?"

"I know she's worried about you. Some email was sent to all parents stating that she and several other teachers at school would be offering extra help to students who are getting a C grade or lower in their classes."

"Really?"

"Yeah. See, she doesn't hate you. If she agreed to do that and give of her time instead of riding her bull-riding machine at home, then you know she doesn't hate you. She's reaching out."

"That's funny."

"Hey, that's my phrase. You can't steal it."

"Hey, let's get off the phone. I should call that number again."

"I'll see you with your brother," Jenna says.

"You're the best, Jenna."

CHAPTER 35

JENNA WAS RIGHT. SOMEONE does answer the phone, the Cedar number.

"Hello?"

"Who's calling please?" a man's voice says. Sounds like he's twenty-something.

"My name's Billy. My brother is Paul. Do you know where he is? Is he okay?"

"Where are you?" the man says.

"In a place past Plum Junction. Bunch of cows around here now. I'm heading toward Cedar. Highway 29."

"You with anyone?"

"Just me. Walking. Trying to go fast."

"I'll pick you up."

"Who are you?"

"Sorry. My name is James."

"How do you know my brother?"

"That's what we need to talk about."

"Is he awake yet? That's all I want to know."

"Yes, he's awake."

I burst into tears.

CHAPTER 36

AN OLD GREY TOYOTA Corolla with side dent pulls up behind me. A guy in nice pants and sweater over a button-down shirt gets out. He opens an umbrella for me. "You must be cold," he says.

"No, I'm good. Got this slicker on and some layers."

"Smart of you to come prepared. But before you ride with me—a complete stranger—I want to assure you of my intentions. First, I brought you a polaroid of you and your brother."

"What?" It's true. He shows me the picture as me and him stand under the open umbrella. A photo of me and Paul at Eagle River.

"Let me phone him right now for you to hear his voice for yourself."

"Sure. I'll hold the umbrella."

James pulls out his phone and dials: "Paul, you won't believe it. I'm with Billy! I know! Yes. I'll put him on the phone."

"Hi, little brother," Paul says to me all groggy.

I burst into tears.

James puts my duffle in the back seat and has me hop in the car.

The nineteen-minute trip seems like forever. I time it on my phone. We arrive at a small one-story cabin. It's off a couple dirt roads. A home by itself in the woods. James parks right in front of it and carries my duffle inside. I follow. My heart's going to explode! . . . My brother!! It's him, he's really here!! Under a blanket!

Eyes closed. Sleeping on a sofa in the center of a room with a fire crackling in a rock fireplace. An open kitchen area behind this main room. Houseplants and pottery all around. Grey cat curled up asleep on Paul. Shaggy dog on the rug beside them. The dog thumps its friendly tail.

James motions for me to follow him. We pass a door on the right. Then a little room that's decorated with paintings and drawings, crafty things all over. James hangs up my slicker on a coat hook in a back laundry area. Shakes out the umbrella in a deep sink. Has me take off my wet sneakers and socks. Sets them by a movable radiator. The dog comes back to say hello to us and wag its tail some more.

"Your brother and I . . . I've been staying full-time with him here these last couple of months, Billy. Your brother needs my help."

"Are you a nurse?"

"No, I wish. I illustrate—draw pictures for kids' books. Can you stay, Billy? Should you call your parents? How did you get here? Oh my gosh, sorry, I have oodles of questions for you. I've been extremely nervous about this. Can't believe you're here!!" He grabs a hold of my shoulders he's so excited.

"I gotta go wake up Paul," I say. "I gotta hear him. He's gotta hear me."

"Of course, I understand," James says. "He's talked about you so much, Billy."

I rush back in. The curled-up cat doesn't budge. Stays right on Paul's chest.

"Paul, I'm here," I say. "Can you hear me? It's me, Billy."

Paul's eyes open. The cat jumps down to rub its side against my leg. Paul sits up. Big smile. Takes him a few seconds before he pulls me in. Hugs me hard. Tears stream down his face. I cry too. Then James starts crying.

"Oh my goodness, we're all a mess," James says with a laugh as he goes and gets us a box of tissues to share.

"I've been dreaming about this day for so long," my brother says.

"Me too," I say as I sit right close to him. He keeps his arm around me. The cat goes from his lap to mine. The dog rests its head on Paul's thigh.

"I thought I had lost you," my brother says.

"Me? What about you?" I say.

James laughs. "How about some tea, you both?"

"Sure," Paul says.

James motions for me to follow him again into the back area.

"He's getting better since the incident," James says quietly.

"The accident you mean?"

"It was no accident."

"Where'd you go?!" Paul calls out to us. "Come on back!"

"Do go sit with your brother while he's up. I'll put the kettle on for tea. Are you hungry?"

"If you have anything, sure," I say.

"Let me put some tea sandwiches together for us all. Please, do go be with him."

"I knew you would wake up after your accident. I just knew it," I say to Paul as I hug him huge.

"Let me just tell you about mom and dad. Before I fall back to sleep. Sorry, I'm so tired. Haven't been myself . . . "

"Okay," I say and sit right close to him.

"They did their best, Mom and Dad."

"Their best?"

"In raising us."

"Okay."

"I don't blame them for throwing me out."

"Okay."

"I wasn't turning into the kid that they wanted. I could be uppity. I started doing dope, staying out late, partying, cussing, keeping personal information from them."

"Okay," I say again.

"I just don't want you to blame them for too much is all. They're parents who want the best for us on their own terms. I still love them even though they reject me—will probably never talk to me again. But I focus on the good times we all had. And there were some. And you. You changed me for the better, Billy."

"I did?"

"Heck yeah. You made me realize that I wanted to care about somebody other than myself. You got me out of my own messed-up little head. I wasn't Mr. Happy then."

James puts another log on the fire before stepping back in the kitchen area.

"I loved how every morning you'd run into my bedroom. Give me the biggest hug. That's what I've missed."

"I loved that too!" I say. "Hugging you!"

"And then before you or me went to bed, if I saw you, you'd hug me real big again and say good night to me. I missed that too."

"Aww," James says.

Paul starts crying again, which makes me start crying again. Then James starts crying as he comes over to us. Grabs a handful of tissues for blowing his nose into.

"I felt real love from you," Paul says.

"And you loved me back," I say. "I felt it."

"Yeah, you taught me about unconditional love. I never forgot that. You'd be surprised what effect you had on me, Billy. Like when Mom and Dad couldn't make one of my baseball games, you'd still show up. Be sitting there all by yourself in the bleachers not talking to anybody. You'd get up and walk around but always stay for the entire game."

"Yes, your memory is coming back," James says after getting control of his sniffling. "You are finally getting better, Paul."

"From the fall?" I say.

"Fall?" Paul says.

"He got beat up," James says.

"Beat up?" I say. "What about the rock climbing? The incident? The fall?" I stand up to look at him.

Paul shakes his head. Looks confused.

"There was no rock-climbing crash," James says as he steps back in the kitchen. "Yeah, I don't remember how long I've been mentally out of it, but they beat me up unconscious."

"Who did?" I ask. "What happened? What are you talking about?"

88

"Three guys. Outside a pub. Right here in our small town," James says as he comes back over to us with mini sandwiches.

"Beat you up? Why?" I ask and start crying all over again.

"Because they saw your brother holding my hand."

"Holding your hand?"

"Look," Paul says. "James is my friend."

"I have a good friend too. Her name is Jenna. I can tell you all about her. I can't wait. There's tons to tell you."

"I've been wanting to talk to you too, Billy—"

"Paul's slowly been recovering from the trauma, the attack," James interrupts. "He has no health insurance. I've been watching over him here as he gets better. Now that he's improving, he's been saying your name in his sleep a lot."

"Yeah, I've had dreams about you too," I say.

"You came all the way here by yourself?" Paul asks me.

I nod.

"Best, most amazing brother anyone could ever have," Paul says.

"I want to come live with you, Paul. Mom and Dad are planning to send me away to some horrible military academy."

"I can try to talk to them, but good chance they'll just hang up on me," Paul says. "I'm sorry I've paved a bad way for you, Billy. Mom and Dad shouldn't think the worst of you because of me."

"It's not your fault," I say.

"Hey, I'm real tired. Will probably fall back asleep, but I want you to know that Mom and Dad don't like how I live. I need to tell you this. Even though I've had some girlfriends, and they've been great, Mom and Dad caught me with Kenny one time. That high school wrestler friend of mine."

"What do you mean? Caught you drinking and smoking?"

"No, more like Mom and Dad realized that me and Kenny liked each other."

"Yeah, I know you really liked him. He became your good friend after Doug moved to Oregon."

"What he's trying to say . . . " James says.

"Is that James is my partner. Another word for that is 'boyfriend.'"

I sit back down.

"I know this is probably confusing and a lot to take in at first meeting. And I know you might react like Mom and Dad did to me when they started to figure things out. But I want you to know that I love you, and I love them too no matter what happens. We all do the best we can. Mom and Dad had a real strict upbringing. You don't know all about their childhoods and what happened to them. I can fill you in later when I get stronger. But you and me can help change that. I mean we can try to give them more love. You've helped me to be more loving, Billy. You can help them with that too."

I turn and give my brother one gigantic hug. "I love you," I say.

Paul smiles before lying back down again and closing his eyes.

That's when I text Jenna. I tell her everything is going to be all right.

CHAPTER 37

"So now what happens?" I ask James the next morning in his car. He's driving us east to a courthouse thirty miles away. Next town over. He wants to talk to an office clerk there. I'm going to help him shop afterwards. He'll be making me and Paul a celebration dinner tonight. A party for the three of us. Said it was for all of us "waking up."

"You really think it's going to work out for me here?" I say.

"I'm hopeful, you bet. Paul has wanted this to happen just as much as you do."

"When will we get an answer?"

"There's a lot to go through still. I really don't know. Weeks? Maybe months before we hear any decision."

"I can't wait that long. I got to escape fast."

"I hope to get more information at the courthouse for you and Paul."

"Can I keep sleeping on your couch with the dog and cat? Like for as long as I can? I liked that. I like them."

"We love that you're here, Billy. Of course. Yes, do snuggle with Odin and Emmy. They love you already. In fact, I have a carpenter friend in town who could build you your own bedroom. Do a house add-on for us. A fast prefab studio shed or something. She's really good."

"Cool."

James's cell phone rings. "Hang on. It's Paul." James answers as he drives . . . "Good morning to you. We're almost there, yes. I didn't want to wake you. Oh, you left a message? . . . Right, they probably won't talk to you . . . at least not yet . . . Okay. Will do." James hangs up.

"Am I in trouble? Does everybody know I've run off? Is Paul in trouble?"

"Paul said he left a phone message for your parents about you. He doesn't want them surprised."

"You mean surprised that me and him are alive and that I'm here?"

"No, more like surprised about when a sheriff will go knocking on their door with papers."

"What does that mean?"

"The papers I have to finish filing online for Paul. The written request that you be able to live with him—us—and go to school here. The sheriff will give your parents a copy of those documents. It's part of the process."

"Wish I could know the future," I say.

"If it helps you to hear," James says, "I truly believe a judge will grant you and Paul your wish to be together. And I don't think your parents will try to prevent it either."

"So what would Paul be called then? What's that term you said last night if I get to stay here?"

"He'd be your guardian. Just like you've been his guardian. You watch over each other . . . Angels, both of you."

"Yeah, that's what I'd call being whole again."